Dreams

and

Nightmares

AT BAY PRESS FICTION ANNUAL:

Dreams and Nightmares

Winnipeg

At Bay Press Fiction Annual
'Dreams and Nightmares'

All selections in this volume are original,
published for the first time here.

All stories copyright © 2015 by their respective authors and artists.

Design and cover artwork
by Matt Joudrey.

At Bay Press fox logo copyright © 2015 At Bay Press.

Published by At Bay Press November 2015.

All rights reserved. The use of any part of this publication, reproduced, transmitted in any form or by any means electronic, mechanical, photocopying, recording or otherwise, or stored in a retrieval system without prior written consent of the publisher-or in the case of photocopying or other reprographic copying, license from the Canadian Copyright Licensing Agency-is an infringement of the copyright law.

This book is a work of fiction. Any similarities to actual events, places or persons, living or dead, is entirely coincidental.

ISBN 978-0-9917610-8-1

Library and Archives Canada cataloguing in
publication is available upon request.

Visit At Bay Press online
atbaypress.com

First Edition

Printed and bound in Canada.

10 9 8 7 6 5 4 3 2 1

Table of Contents

Kwi'Lanx: The Feasting Season by Lucy Haché 1

In the Trees by Anders Homenick 9

Common Housefly by M C Joudrey 15

True Dreams by Scott A. Ford 25

The Woman I Can't See by Van Kunder 31

Within this House by Michael Joyal 41

Kwi'Lanx: The Feasting Season
by Lucy Haché

Sun shone through vibrant green leaves as wind swayed them, giving my surroundings a flickering, shimmering feel. I could smell the undertone of the soil's muskiness. I was in a forest clearing, cradled on a bed of moss. Thankfully too, for my bones were old. Yet the ever-present ache was noticeably absent. I sat up carefully, moved my toes and fingers and tentatively stretched my arms above me. No pain. I pushed myself up onto my feet and gazed around in wonder. The place was familiar to me, yet I didn't know how I arrived there. Was I dead? Was this what they called heaven? No, it couldn't be. I spent my childhood here, before the government relocated us to the reserve. It was as close to heaven as you could get on earth.

I was in Ba'as – the sheltered place. I looked up in time to see a flash of feathers slice through the air with precision. The black wisp settled on the lower branches of an ancient cedar and called, *xalah*! It sounded like a chuckle. It was Raven, Trickster, Story Keeper. To some, Raven is considered a bad omen. For us, he is the Bringer of Light; stealing sun from those who coveted it and releasing it into the sky so that plants might grow and creatures might thrive. Like all creatures, Raven is to be respected. He is an ancestor. There was a time when animals could take off their feathers or fur and walk with humans. Although the animals no longer transform, they are still our kin. Or at least they are to those of us who still believe the old ways.

Lost in thought, I didn't notice someone had entered the clearing with me. I turned to find a tall man regarding me quizzically. He was handsome with long black hair and a black robe. He was neither young, nor old.

"*Yo, Wiksas, Nugwa'am Gwa'wina,*" he said, with a voice like sweet laughter in my own language.

How long had it been since I last heard it? No one speaks it anymore. They call it a dying language.

"*Nugwa'am Ada,*" I replied.

He laughed as he said, "I know." We continued to speak in our language. "*Pusḵa'mas* – are you hungry?" he asked. "I have some *kawas* to share." I accepted the strip of dried smoked sockeye gratefully.

"Come with me, I'm going to *hamsa*–pick berries," said Gwa'wina. My eyes brightened with excitement. How long had it been since I last picked berries? Arthritis had kept my hands from working properly for longer than I could remember. I had been forced to settle for buying berries from the grocery store.

Berry season was my favorite time of year. First would come the gold and red salmonberries: vibrant, bittersweet and juicy. Next to ripen were thimbleberries: deep red and sweet with an earthy spiciness. Next came huckleberries and wild blueberries: tiny but bursting with refreshing tangy juiciness. Finally came the salal berries: earthy and very sweet. My hands would be stained deep purple for days afterwards. We truly lived in a land of abundance. Why did we ever allow ourselves to be taken away from the land that gave us life?

"Follow me," said Gwa'wina. He led me through the forest, passing bracken fern, sitka spruce, douglas fir, cedar and salal. Here it was darker than the clearing, with giant cedar and spruce reaching for the sky. Yet, it was no less vibrant. I may have been dead, but I couldn't remember the last time I felt so alive. The forest's embrace uplifted me.

We walked for some time without talking. All the while I knew where we were going. This forest had been my playground. After a while, I could see the forest ended abruptly, as if the world itself ended. We continued to walk towards the end of the world, through the curtain of conifers onto an expanse of desolation.

Where once stood the great trees—the medicine givers, the shelter providers—now remained an ugly scar on the earth. I knew this place too, even without my old friends the trees. This place was a part of me. But where there were once cedars and spruce there were now jagged stumps. Trees of lesser value were also cut. Discarded in heaps and bleached by the sun and rain, they looked like piles of bones. In some places the earth was scorched black where they had burned discarded timber. The desolation was as far as my eyes could see. Tears swelled. Our lives had revolved around reciprocal relationships with each other and with the forest and with the sea. This land belonged to us in the same way we belonged to it.

So strong was my turmoil that I had forgotten about Gwa'wina. A chuckle brought me out of my thoughts and I turned sharply to glare at him. He looked back at me with a sly smile on his face and said, "I want to show you something."

He walked onto the clear-cut area and I followed, not sure what else to do. We walked for a while and I began to notice different plants around me: fragrant pink swords of blooming fireweed, vibrant orange-red bunchberry, fresh, bright green salmonberry bush and young alder. There were also many *gwadum*, huckleberries. The spindly green branches were heavy with the vibrant red baubles. We stopped suddenly and Gwa'wina handed me a cedar-bark *kalatsi*, a basket to fill with huckleberries. I don't know where he got it from...perhaps he was carrying it the whole time.

We began harvesting the berries, stopping to eat some from time to time. The berries burst in my mouth, their tangy sweetness brought me back to my childhood and a smile found its way onto my face. My mind forgot where we were and focused on the task of gathering. Peace filled me and hours passed us by. Soon my *kalatsi* was full.

"What are these berries for?" I asked Gwa'wina, curious about what we would do with so many.

With a crooked smile and a gleam in his eyes he replied, "*Kwi'lanx*, the feasting season."

The ambulance siren blared through my consciousness. No, not heaven. A dream. As reality settled in so did the ache in my bones and the loneliness in my soul. I could smell the harsh odor of chemical cleaner and hear the constant hum of medical equipment.

"How the hell did I get here?" I thought, grumpily. My head was pounding and I could hear the annoying chatter of nurses and hospital workers in the hallway.

"Are you awake?" A tall, middle-aged nurse with blonde hair stood in the doorway with pity on her face.

I don't need your pity, I thought, but nodded my head painfully in reply. "Why am I here?" I croaked, not really wanting to know.

"Alcohol toxicity. You almost killed yourself this time, you know," she scolded.

I looked away without reply. I stopped drinking 15 years ago, but a lifetime of losing everything that mattered sometimes overwhelmed me. At least I still had my language, but without anyone to speak to other than Gwa'wina in my dreams, it was not much comfort. In many ways, my waking life was a nightmare I couldn't escape.

"We've contacted your family to let them know you're here," said the nurse, throwing open my curtains to let the sun in. I covered my eyes with the blanket and thought about my kids. I had given birth to three beautiful babies. I loved them dearly, but I was unable to protect them from the same abuse I had experienced at that wretched school. If I had kept them home, I would have gone to jail. We all lost ourselves in alcohol; it was the only way we knew how to forget the pain. Thankfully the horrible residential schools were outlawed before they could claim my grandchildren too. Still, the cycle of abuse had begun. My kids and grandkids were busy with their own lives now. I didn't expect them to come see me, but they still provided some joy in my long life.

On my third day in the hospital I was told I could go home the next day. I didn't have much to look forward to back home, but at least I would get some of my dignity back. I was tired of having people feed me, wash me and poke me with needles. What happened to my pride? Respect was once the pillar of our culture. Our ceremonies existed so that we could give thanks to the natural and spiritual world for the abundance provided us, and so that we could share that abundance with others. We once were stewards of the land, taking care of it so that it would take care of us. *Now everything comes from the damn grocery store*, I thought bitterly.

I remembered the last thing Gwa'wina said to me in my dream: *"Kwi'lanx."* Spring, summer and fall were spent harvesting and preparing food so that winter would be spent feasting and celebrating. Winter was desolate, but because of the hard work of the harvest season it was a time of abundance and celebration. We didn't just survive the winter, we thrived.

On my last day in the hospital, I was sitting in the afternoon sun that was leaching through the window. I was watching a pair of stellar-jays outside. They were having a heated argument about something. I imagined they were arguing about what to have for dinner.

"You have a visitor," came a voice from the doorway. I turned as the tall blonde nurse stepped aside to allow my visitor to enter the room. "This young lady is from the school in your community." The girl was about 12 years old, with long black hair, bright eyes and a crooked smile that reminded me of someone. I'd seen her on the reserve before. Her gran was my cousin Mary, a kind woman who had sadly passed away years ago.

The girl sat down on a chair beside my bed and spoke to me brightly. *"Gilakas'la Ada, nugwa'am* Lily." A smile warmed my face as Lily greeted me in our language. I couldn't remember the last time I heard those words in my waking life.

"My gran was your cousin Mary, my mom is Jane. Do you remember me?"

"Yes, I remember you sweetheart. You used to visit me with your mama when you were a little one. Where did you learn to speak Kwak'wala?" I asked.

"My Gran taught me that bit before she passed away. But that's all I know," Lily offered with a shy grin and a shrug of her shoulders. "I want to learn about the old ways, and how to speak our language." She looked at me, eyes pleading, "Please, will you teach me?"

I remembered the taste of huckleberries. Thoughts of pain and loss faded from my mind and were replaced by a mixture of hope and pride. I held her hand in mine and smiled.

"*Ade*—my dear, I will teach you. The first word we will learn is *kwi'lanx*, the feasting season."

In the Trees
by Anders Homenick

AT BAY PRESS FICTION ANNUAL

DREAMS AND NIGHTMARES

AT BAY PRESS FICTION ANNUAL

DREAMS AND NIGHTMARES

Common Housefly
by M C Joudrey

Birds had torn the black plastic bag wide open. An unrecognizable mix of rotting meat and vegetables spewed forth. The black-feathered scavengers gorged themselves on the remains, leaving a scattered, sticky residue on the sidewalk that attracted the flies.

Dozens of flies had arrived, their sensory receptors able to find the sickly scent on the air. They skidded into the liquefied waste and rubbed their forelegs together in anticipation. The flies greedily lapped at the juices of decay.

A man stepped out of his garage and tried to collect the mess into a fresh bag, nearly stepping on all the flies that speedily flew out from under his feet. One fly in particular waited until the last moment before taking flight as it drank as much of the ooze as possible.

The fly went in search of its next meal, stopping on a fencepost for a moment to deposit feces. The fly followed the scent of something new that excited its senses. When its red eyes located the deceased pigeon, the fly's tiny brain sent a message to its mesothorax and the fly drove towards the prize.

It landed on the rotting pigeon corpse which had been dead for some time. Other flies had located her remains and were already feeding and depositing excrement as they did. The carrion was lying in the middle of an alley. As a vehicle drove by, the fly was startled and took flight. The other flies however couldn't ignore the hunger gnawing at them. They remained with the corpse and the vehicle passed right over top of them.

The fly was aimless in flight for a while, as nothing of interest could be seen or smelled. The fly entered a crowd of humans moving in various chaotic directions. Irritated, the fly perched atop a man's head where it remained for mere seconds before being shooed away by the man's hand.

The simple housefly picked up a scent that drove it nearly mad with desire as it navigated towards the source with unwavering concentration. Many humans were seated outdoors on a patio. The fly found a perch on the perimeter railing and used its wide-angle receptors to view the discovery. It watched as humans brought other humans food. Most of the food appeared dry in nature and was of little interest to the fly, until a human came through the restaurant door carrying a rust coloured liquid.

The fly could not control its urge to know more about this liquid with such a tantalizing aroma. The fly landed on the rim of the bowl and approached slowly, leg by leg by leg, until it was almost touching the liquid with its forelegs.

The human carrying the food made a sudden movement and the fly lost its traction. It fell into the viscous liquid which was warm and utterly delicious, but the fly realized almost instantly the peril of its situation. It was drowning, yet the flavour of the liquid was so intoxicating it did not attempt to escape.

As the fly sunk below the surface, a metal object entered and scooped the fly up out of the bowl, along with a good portion of the liquid. The fly was able to slowly find its footing but it was too late. Its compound eyes watched in multiplied horror as it was hoisted upwards and deposited into the mouth of a human.

The fly tried to take flight but its wings were rendered useless by the liquid and it failed to escape its doom. The human swallowed the liquid with the fly and began to choke. Terror filled the tiny mind of the fly as it was forced back up the human's throat, then down and up again, until finally the turmoil stopped.

The human had fallen to the ground, a victim of death by choking. The fly had been completely consumed, drawn into the man's stomach.

Both fly and human were dead. Still, another human tried to revive the man and laid him on his back, thrusting against the dead man's chest and then breathing into his mouth.

After a few minutes of this, the dead man came back to life. He sat up and coughed violently, spewing digested food and bile from his mouth. The man looked up at the humans, confused.

Many of the humans made noises with their mouths, but the man could not understand these noises. He held his hands out in front of him and rubbed them together. They looked like the hands of a human. He could not see with the perspective he once had and the angles he could normally observe could no longer be perceived.

The man stood and jumped up and down. He could not take flight. Nor could he find his other two legs. The man made a noise with his vocal chords and shook all over in fear from the sound that escaped his mouth. The man looked at the other humans who were watching him, mouths agape.

The human who had revived him put his hand on his shoulder and made a noise with his mouth. The man could not understand at all and pushed him away, causing the other human to knock over a table and plates full of food and drinks onto the ground.

The man fell to the sidewalk and started to lap up the spilled liquids with his tongue. His arms and hands were wet with various juices and the man rubbed them together to clean them and licked his hands with his tongue. Many of the other humans watched in disgust and made more noises with their mouths.

The man looked up from the ground and realized he was not safe. The other humans watched as he got up and started to run. None of the onlookers had realized what they had actually witnessed; the instantaneous death of man and fly that produced an aberration of natural selection. What remained was the body of a man and the mind of a fly.

The fly-man ran along the sidewalk erratically, with no clear thought or intention. He ran into other people, knocking some over. Others made loud noises at him with their mouths that the fly-man did not understand.

Crazed with fear, the fly-man ran into the street and was struck by a car. The pain was great and the fly-man could not comprehend what had happened to him. His injuries were not enough to immobilize him and the fly-man started running again aimlessly, until he found refuge in an alley behind a garbage dumpster. The smell from the dumpster was comforting and he felt safe in its presence. He looked over his strange body. His primitive brain was only starting to register his new appendages and diminished visual and auditory faculties.

His mind told him he was hungry but his stomach did not seem to agree. Still, driven by instinct the fly-man climbed into the dumpster and found many wonderful treats to consume. When he had consumed his fill, the fly-man defecated in the dumpster and climbed out.

He walked now instead of ran, which seemed like a less taxing approach to movement and allowed him to react in time to the various obstacles around him.

On a crowded sidewalk, the fly-man tried to move with the ebb and flow of traffic and was pleased to find he could do so. It was strange how quickly he became accustomed to not being able to fly. However, other things such as his appetite were still unmanageable.

The fly-man was beginning to notice the difference between the human sexes. A female human was walking a dog in front of him and the fly-man had a sudden urge to follow the female and the dog. He did not understand the urge, nor could he control it. He didn't want to.

The female human and dog stopped walking, and the dog hunched and began to defecate on the sidewalk. Fresh feces landed on the sidewalk and the fly-man watched with excitement. When the dog had completed its task, the female human took an object from her pocket and began to crouch down towards the feces.

The fly-man could not allow the female human to enjoy the feces before him, so he dropped to his knees and grabbed at the feces to claim it as his own. The female human recoiled in horror and a loud, high pitched noise escaped from her mouth. The fly-man did not understand what was happening and became afraid.

The fly-man stood up quickly and grabbed at the woman, inadvertently touching her breasts. This seemed to excite the fly-man and he continued to paw at her breasts and face without understanding why he felt compelled to do so.

A police officer who had heard the noises approached and subdued the fly-man, binding his arms in what the fly-man believed to be some type of metal claw that could not be broken, no matter how hard he tried. The police officer put the fly-man into his vehicle and drove off. Confused, the fly-man kicked and shook violently. The police officer made abrupt vocal noises at him but still the fly-man comprehended nothing. All he wanted to do was eat and fornicate and couldn't understand why he was being punished for something so harmless.

After many different humans looked and pointed at him and made strange noises while observing him for some time, the fly-man was put into a cage of sorts and was held there for many more days. There was a positive aspect of his confinement, which was the food. It was wet and delicious and the fly-man ate heartily. He began to love being served food every day.

Still, he was often taken from his cage where other humans would make noises at him and look at him in strange ways. Eventually the other humans would return the fly-man to his cage and he would be served more wet food.

One day the fly-man fell ill and vomited all over the floor of his cage. Normally, the fly-man would be instinctually drawn to eating the vomit but on this day he had no such desire. He was losing his appetite. Wet food would be given to him but he would not eat it.

Eventually he grew fatigued and lost weight. His eyes were sunken and his skin began to wrinkle on his hands and body. He was severely dehydrated and before long, his breathing became laboured and he took on a fever. He was confused and wanted to escape and fly away but he remembered he no longer had wings and he was too weak to move at all.

*****

The fly-man died one evening shortly after his illness took hold. The specialists who had tried to save his life did not know what had caused his death. They believed that he suffered from various mental illnesses, but the fly-man was not in their care long enough for them to offer any concrete diagnosis. One doctor thought he suffered from delusions and schizophrenia. Another thought he was simply illiterate, mute and had abused drugs for too long. None were sure, but the fly-man was without a doubt the most curious patient they ever had at the institution.

In light of the unusual circumstances surrounding his death, an autopsy was performed. It was determined the man died from a combination of Cholera and unattributed brain atrophy. A half-digested common housefly carrying the Cholera virus was found in the man's stomach, among other unusual matter. Everyone found it to be a very strange case indeed.

True Dreams
by Scott A. Ford

| True Dreams | Nº 1 | *"Beasts"* |

"The warehouse was surely about to collapse entirely. But as I heard yet another beast swoop down, I knew that we couldn't leave yet either."

True Dreams   Nº 2   *"Creatures"*

" Such a strange mix of calm and dread. We all knew that we couldn't let them touch us. But I was paralyzed and couldn't move away, even as one floated within inches of my leg."

True Dreams   Nº 3   *"Annex"*

"I didn't know that this annex of the school even existed. Nobody did, by the looks of it. And yet, from just down the hall echoed the muffled sounds of a class in progress."

True Dreams   N° 4   *"Elevator"*

"We should have known better than to take the elevator. It was a paint-peeled wooden box and it didn't even reach the sides of the shaft."

True Dreams   Nº 5   *"Theatre"*

"I had a feeling they were my friends even though I didn't recognize any of them. Friends or not, there was nothing they could do to help me. I collapsed in the streets and the lights went out."

The Woman I Can't See
by Van Kunder

And even as I sit beside him, mind racing, shoulders hanging awkwardly in a mix of self-consciousness and torment, the only sound I hear is a shrill white noise.

I perch to his right, tapping my hand against the taut sheets of his bed. I try not to look at him. I try to not really look at anything. My tapping fingers are the heedless result of the distraught nervousness trying to leave my body.

I stare at the skin across his knuckles, trying to get lost in the labyrinth of lines and grooves that live there. I've never really looked at his hands so closely.

I know I should weave my fingers through his, but I can't do it. I can't interrupt the soothing rhythm of my fingertips. I'm scared that if I stop, I'll shatter into a million pieces on top of him, and the thought of everyone else in the room witnessing my unraveling makes my shoulders cower even more.

The room is swollen with people. I can feel the heavy presence of my mother and sister somewhere behind me. I know I'm not the focus of their attention, but the alien setting has me peeling out of my skin with uneasiness. There are other relatives in the room, each one trying not to breathe too loudly. It makes me even more self-conscious of my own lungs' raspy intake.

But there is something else in the room. Something with leaden mitts presses against the chest of each of us, stealing a little bit of breath with each exhale. I don't know what I should be feeling, but the only feeling I can cling to is Embarrassment.

I'm the last to arrive to his room. I missed everyone else sitting awkwardly with him, eschewing any possibility of knowing how to carry myself. On the drive over, the only thing I could do was stare out the window as the sun peeked out over the horizon, trying not to think or to feel.

The ringing I hear is the memory of the phone call. It was too early for the phone to ring. My mind seems to have hiccupped on the ringing of the telephone when they called us to tell us he was dead.

The walls of his room compress me with their foreignness. Even as the sunlight spills between the blinds to decorate the bland walls with rows of dancing light, everything looks dull.

Somehow my gaze has meandered from the creases in his hands to the inside of his elbow where tubes and tape pull at his skin. They disappear into his body, red and clear liquids winding around a machine. I begin gnawing on my lip as I realize my eyes are crawling up to his shoulder. I don't want to look at his face. I can't look at his face.

I'm not ready.

The staples in his neck abruptly halt my wandering eyes. The dark purple skin surrounding them looks tender and painful. Staples don't belong in a body. They squish out from his skin, begging to be plucked free. I feel my chest's first spasm, wishing I could rip the staples from him to soothe his ache.

Like he could feel the ache.

Two days ago, we sat around a tiny table in an even tinier room. They had just stapled him closed. There, they told us he had two weeks to live and that there was nothing more they could do. And they had to rip him open, mangling his once strong body just to make the determination that it was hopeless. I looked to my mother for more information; answers—an explanation—anything. But the guttural cries that burst from my sister made the room spin. All my questions got tangled in the violent whirling, and I've been whirling ever since.

Two days.

I take a deep breath as my eyes squeeze shut.

A fist tightens around my throat, the same familiar mitt that has made its presence known since I walked in. I try to swallow, but my tongue feels too big for my mouth. I turn from him and let my eyes rest on the sunshine trying to cleanse the room.

I wish I had never come into this room.

I barely recognize him. His jaw is slack, pulling away from his face in a gesture I have never seen him make. His powerful features are sunken and meek. His eyelids are barely open, but their tiny slits reveal his powder blue eyes set against the blue shade the whites of his eyes have turned. I can barely tell the two colours apart.

His poor lips are cracked and dry, remnants of a tiny damp sponge caught in the dry skin – a token from the wine-soaked sponge my mother pressed against his lips last night as the hour ticked closer to her birthday. Even then, part of me hadn't given up. I questioned if the tiny drip of alcohol would somehow interfere with his pain medication.

Like it really mattered.

I feel myself pulling into the comfort of Embarrassment's embrace. As I stare at his limp body beneath me, I can feel it carving an imprint onto my soul. Something within me tightens, darkens, and begins to mold. The bones in my fingers and toes seem to stiffen while my chest cracks and splits from the inexplicable pressure inside me. But now that I'm looking at him, I can't look away.

My sister's shoulder bumps into me, jarring my paralysis. She collapses beside me onto the bed, her skinny arms against his chest. Her cries have become so familiar to me they're almost soothing. They feel like a release, even though they escape her throat and not mine. As she bellows on top of him, I catch her whispering weeping words of love and affection to his lifeless corpse.

Embarrassment wraps a gnarly arm around me as I watch her.

I have to back away. I feel suffocated watching her and yet relieved to be free from the malicious hypnotism his dead body cast on me. Death has a magnetic pull and everyone in the room seems to be pulsating with its rotten energy.

My sister's faint whispers mix with the ringing in my ears, goading and poking me. Each word sticks into my spine like tiny flecks of electricity, forcing me back into the corner of the room. I feel like everyone is expecting me to say something, express something, but the grip on my shoulder is too strong.

The sun spills over my face. I crumple down into a chair tucked under the window. Its frame melds with mine, supporting my frail bones. I can't tell where the chair begins and where I end.

I imagine Embarrassment floating over to stand beside me, as Death scowls at me from beside the steel bed frame, reaching for me with heavy gloves.

My gaze floats across the room until my eyes settle on my mother's face. Despite the months of wear, she is still beautiful. Death's magnetism has aged her, but her anguish holds a tone of relief.

He had been struggling. He had been in pain. And his guilt of leaving her behind ate at her soul just as much as it did his.

Relief places a gentle hand on her shoulders.

She stands beside his bed. Her dark hair falls in front of her face, seemingly hugging her in a curtain of protection. She looks vulnerable: young and weathered at the same time, her eyelashes are wet and her neck is strained as I recognize Death's grip around her. Still, Relief keeps her steady.

Everyone in the room seems to fall away, fading into the pale walls. Even with my terrified sister lying on the corpse, it's only my mother I can see.

What does this mean for us now? What will she do?

She carefully lowers herself onto the bed next to him, picking up his heavy hand and placing it between hers. She moves his dark hair from his forehead and seems to look past the ugly, unfamiliar grimace his face has adopted.

She leans into him, pressing her lips against his still ones.

I catch the spasm in her neck and quickly feel the dread pooling into my stomach. It cuts through me before I can look away.

Relief grips her shoulder tightly.

A cry bursts from her throat before she can pull her lips from his. She tries to search his eyes, but they don't find hers. They will never look at her again. They will never crinkle with a smile again.

I look down at my hands in my lap. My palms stare back at me.

I should have held his hand.

Embarrassment's paw gently pats my back, but I can't help but shudder.

I close my eyes, drinking in the redness of my closed eyelids as the sun washes over me. The smell of roses explodes in my nose and I inhale deeply, trying to focus on their scent.

He sent the roses for her. They aren't roses symbolizing the sadness and finality of death. They are roses that symbolize the immense love a man felt for his wife before he died, and even past his death.

I open my eyes to look at them, to see what he wanted to give her today since it's her birthday. But their crispness and vivid colour don't match the room. They fight Death's pull with their overwhelming beauty.

Another being stands with the roses, wiping her delicate hands over each petal, but I can't identify her. I can't see her properly from beneath Death's shadow and Embarrassment's slung arm where I silently sit.

I look around me and notice every other pair of eyes has turned from my mother's shaking and crying body. They all settle somewhere on the twelve bouquets surrounding the room. It's as if the Woman I Can't See fills the void between us, pressing herself against Death's hulking presence.

I realize the invasion I feel for watching my parents say their final goodbye is felt throughout the full, pale room.

My sister collapses beside me, clinging to my arm and crying against it. I'm too numb to comfort her, so I let her cry against me. A part of me feels cruel for it, but the cruelty is less painful than allowing myself to succumb to her cries. If I wrap an arm around her, I'll only absorb her pain into mine.

The room spills into a formal line of bodies, each one pausing in front of the dead body and touching it in some way. A chorus of goodbyes fills my ears as I watch from the corner of the room.

No one looks at me.

And I don't say goodbye.

I somehow float out of the room; unaware of who is holding my arm and uncertain if Death, Embarrassment, Relief and the Woman I Can't See follow us. I scan the hallway for my sister's light hair, alarmed when I can't hear her familiar cries. But the hallway is eerily quiet. We are all cried out.

I look back up the hallway to where his room is. It feels strange for us all to leave him in there alone. What will happen to him? Who will take him?

A hand searches for mine but I quickly pull my fists up into my sweater to conceal them. I don't want to touch anyone. I don't want to feel the pulse of death that connects us together.

I don't want to feel anything.

But I do feel a familiar hand on my shoulder. The hand of Embarrassment walks the hallway with me.

The cold air is harsh as we leave the hospital. The sun's warm light is deceiving as it bounces off the snow. Unwilling to linger in the icy temperatures too long, everyone disperses into their own vehicles, the roses taking their own van back home. It's as if they don't want to be tainted by Death's magnetism, too regal in their proclamation of love.

As the van's doors close, I spot her behind the glass – the Woman I Can't See. She too, is unable to stay back in the pale room.

I don't hear my mother turn the key to start the engine, but somehow I end up in the front seat beside her, my sister coiled into herself behind us. She is older than me, but she is more breakable in her gentleness and sensitivity. Out of the three of us, I know she will howl into her pillow the most. I mentally begin searching for my headphones back at the house.

I hope the roses and the Woman I Can't See settle in my sister's room.

I know Embarrassment will end up in mine.

As the car begins to move, my thoughts are diverted back to the pale room where we left him. Is he alone? Has the taut blanket been pulled over his head as his body is wheeled down the hall by a stranger?

Does Death walk beside him into the hospital's bowels?

I want to ask my mother. I want to know what happens to his body. But when I turn to look at her, I catch the quiver in her lip as her long thin hands grip the steering wheel.

I know she is wondering the same things I am.

The white roads are barren as we drive home. The snowy fields seem to bow to us, hanging their heads in remorse. Everything blurs together like a white-out winter storm.

My mother's hand falls to my knee as she lowers the music she had turned on to drown out all our thoughts.

"I used to think this song was about me and your dad..." she starts, clearing her throat. "I used to think that we would make it through anything..." Her voice hangs at the end, but this time she doesn't cry. As I stare at her, I realize something around her has changed. She turns from me and clicks a button on the stereo, restarting the song from the beginning.

I lean forward and turn the volume up, unable to pull my eyes away from the sight around her. The Woman I Can't See has her arms wrapped around my mother's body, gently stretching her own hands over my mother's as they grip the steering wheel to guide us home.

Within this House
by Michael Joyal

Inside this house of ours, strangers guard the darkest heart.

Maybe someday if I tell myself enough,
I'll be falling around you.

The pieces that they take from
you are the ones you cannot hide.

Contributors

Alana Brooker Senior editor for At Bay Press. She received her Bachelor of Arts degree from the University of Manitoba and her Bachelor of Laws degree from Osgoode Hall at York University. Ms. Brooker was called to the Bar of Ontario in 2007.

Scott A. Ford Artist, designer, and storyteller. The first issue of his independent graphic novel series, *Romulus + Remus*, was nominated for the 2012 Manitoba Book Awards (Best Illustrated Book of the Year). Scott recently graduated from the University of Manitoba with an Honours Degree in Fine Arts. He has since showcased a new body of illustrative work at the Edge Gallery.

Lucy Haché British Columbia based writer and adventurer of First Nations/Métis and Scottish/Irish descent. She grew up in Tsulquate, a small First Nations Community on the Northern tip of Vancouver Island. Much of her childhood was spent in the forest or on the sea. When she's not surrounded by nature she writes about it. She also writes about contemporary and historical First Nations issues.

Anders Homenick Winnipeg photographer. His photographs reflect his approach to life, love, and friendship. He is always searching for new experiences, people and their lifestyles, at home and abroad, to capture with his lens. His methods include using vintage cameras and shooting on film. His work can be seen at friendshipfilms.ca

M C Joudrey Canadian writer, artist and 2015 Manitoba Book Award nominee (John Hirsch Award). Mr. Joudrey is also a bookbinder and a number of his pieces are held in galleries all over the world. Much of his writing is held in permanent legislative and national government collections. His work can be seen at mattjoudrey.com

Michael Joyal Winnipeg based artist. He recently spent one year drawing a single piece of art for each day, culminating in the show '365 Days Before I Sleep' at Cre8ery Gallery. He has also produced the comic zines 'CrUDE' and 'Disturb'. Mr. Joyal received his BFA from the Nova Scotia College of Art & Design. His work can been seen at leadvitamins.blogspot.com

Van Kunder Fantasy and science fiction writer from Winnipeg. She has also published work exploring dance, music, theatre and culture. As the art director of SANDBOX magazine, Van was one of four individuals who brought the world of fashion, culture and lifestyle to print in the Canadian Prairies. Her work can be seen at vankunder.com

OTHER TITLES FROM AT BAY PRESS

Available now:

The Edge 125 Pacific Avenue
Various contributors
Non-Fiction
Paperback
ISBN: 9780987966551
$15.99

At Bay Press Fiction Annual: Jilted Love
Fiction Anthology
Paperback
ISBN: 9780991761005
$9.99

Woman: An Anthology
Fiction Anthology
Hardcover
ISBN: 9780991761036
$29.99

Charleswood Road: Stories
M C Joudrey
Fiction Stories
Hardcover
ISBN: 9780991761043
$22.99

Forthcoming:

Clouds
Lucy Haché
Illustrations by Michael Joyal
Fiction
Paperback
ISBN 9780991761074
$24.95
Releases: Fall 2015